HANS CHRISTIAN ANDERSEN'S

THUMBELINA

ADAPTED AND ILLUSTRATED BY

DEMI

DODD MEAD & COMPANY

NEW YORK

To
E. V. STEBBINS SWEENEY

Printed in The United States of America by Horowitz/Rae

Design and art direction by Barbara DuPree Knowles

1 2 3 4 5 6 7 8 9 10

LIBRARY OF CONGRESS CATALOGING-IN-PUBLICATION DATA
Demi.   Hans Christian Andersen's Thumbelina.
   SUMMARY: A tiny girl no bigger than a thumb is stolen by
a great, ugly toad, and subsequently has many adventures
and makes many animal friends before finding the perfect
mate in a warm and beautiful southern land.
   [1. Fairy tales]   I. Andersen, H.C. (Hans Christian),
1805-1875. Tommelise.   II. Title.   III. Title:
Thumbelina.
PZ8.D3994Han   1988   [E]   87-19054
ISBN 0-396-09241-1

THERE ONCE WAS a woman who wanted to have a tiny little child. She did not know where to get one, so she went to a fairy.

"I should so much like to have a tiny little child, but I don't know where to get one. Can you please help me?" she asked.

"Oh, yes!" said the fairy. "Here is a barleycorn, but it is not the kind the farmer plants or feeds to the chickens. Put it in a flower pot and you will see something happen."

The woman thanked the fairy and then hurried home to plant the barleycorn. Immediately, up sprouted a large tulip—its petals still closed.

"How beautiful!" exclaimed the woman, as she kissed the bud. The flower burst open and, in the center, there sat a tiny little girl—quite trim and very pretty. She was scarcely half a thumb in height, so the woman called her Thumbelina.

A polished walnut shell served Thumbelina as a cradle, the blue
petals of a violet were her mattress, and a rose leaf her quilt.
There she lay at night, but during the day she played about on the
table where the woman had put a shallow bowl of water ringed
with flowers. In the middle floated a great tulip petal on which
Thumbelina sat. She sailed from one side of the bowl to the
other, rowing herself with oars made of two white horsehairs.

One night when she was lying in her pretty little bed, an old
toad crept in through a broken pane in the window. She was very
ugly, clumsy, and clammy; she hopped onto the table where
Thumbelina lay asleep.

"*This* would make a beautiful wife for my son," said the toad.
She took up the walnut shell and hopped out through the
window into the garden.

There flowed a great wide stream, with slippery, muddy banks, where the toad lived with her son. Ugh! How ugly and clammy he was, just like his mother!

"Croak, croak, croak!" was all he could say when he saw the pretty little girl in the walnut shell.

"Don't talk so loud, or you'll wake her," said the old toad. "We will put her on a broad lily leaf in the stream. That will be quite an island for her. She can't run away from us there."

The leaf farthest away was the largest. So the old toad swam to it with Thumbelina.

When Thumbelina woke up the next morning and saw where she was, she began to cry bitterly, for on every side of the great green leaf was water. She could not get to land.

The toads came out to greet her.

"Here is my son," said the old toad. "You shall marry him and live in great magnificence down under the swamp."

"Croak, croak, croak!" was all that the son could say.

Then they swam away and left Thumbelina alone on the great leaf where she wept. She did not want to live with the clammy toad or marry her ugly son.

Under the water the little fishes had seen and heard the old toad quite plainly. They put up their heads to see the little girl and thought her too pretty to live with two ugly toads. No, that must not happen. They circled the green stalk that supported the leaf on which Thumbelina was sitting and nibbled the stem in two.

Away floated the leaf down the stream, bearing Thumbelina far beyond the reach of the toads. On she sailed, past several towns, and the little birds sitting in the bushes saw her and sang, "What a pretty little girl!" The leaf floated farther and farther away.

A butterfly fluttered above her, then settled on the leaf. Thumbelina was delighted. The toads could not reach her now, and it was so lovely where she was travelling. The sun shining on the water made it sparkle like silver. She took off her sash, and tied one end round the butterfly. The other she fastened to the leaf so that it glided along faster than ever.

A great cockchafer flying past caught sight of Thumbelina.
He swooped down, picked up the tiny girl, and flew off with her to a
tree. Oh, dear! How terrified poor little Thumbelina felt! The cockchafer
sat her down on a large green leaf, gave her nectar from the flowers to eat
and told her that she was very pretty—although not in the *least* like a
cockchafer. Later on, other cockchafers came to pay call. They examined
Thumbelina closely.

One remarked, "Why she has only two legs! How terrible!"

"And she has no feelers!" cried another.

"How ugly she is!" said all the lady chafers.

When the cockchafer who had stolen her heard all the ladies saying
she was ugly, he began to think so too, and would not keep her. He flew
down from the tree with her and put her on a daisy. There she sat and
wept, because she felt so ugly. Even the cockchafer would have nothing
to do with her.

The whole summer and fall little Thumbelina lived alone
in the great wood. She wove a bed for herself out of grass
and hung it under a clover leaf, so that she was protected
from the rain. She gathered nectar from the flowers for
food and drank the dew from the leaves every morning.

Then came winter—the long, cold winter. The birds who had sung so
sweetly about her flew away. The trees shed their leaves and the flowers
died. Poor little Thumbelina! She was terribly cold. Her clothes were
ragged and surely she would freeze to death. It began to snow, and every
snowflake that fell was to her as a whole shovelful thrown on one of us,
for we are so big and she was only an inch high. She wrapped herself in
a maple leaf, but it was full of holes and gave her no warmth.

Thumbelina wandered outside the great wood into a large cornfield. But the corn had been harvested and only dry, bare stubble was left standing in the frozen ground. All at once she came across the door of a field mouse, who lived quite warm and snug in a little hole under some cornstalks. Poor little Thumbelina knocked on the door to beg for a piece of barley; she had not had anything to eat for the last two days.

"Poor little creature!" said the field mouse, for she was a kind old thing at heart. "Come into my warm room and share my dinner."

Thumbelina pleased her. "As far as I am concerned," she said, "you may spend the winter with me, but you must keep my room clean and tidy and tell me stories, for I like that very much."

The tiny girl did all the field mouse asked and remarkably well, too.

One day the field mouse said, "My neighbor is coming to visit me today. He is in better circumstances than I am, and he wears a fine black velvet coat. If you could only marry him, you would be well provided for. He can't see you, for he is blind, so you must tell him the prettiest stories you know."

He came and paid them a visit in his black velvet coat, but
Thumbelina was not at all interested in him, for he was a *mole*.

"He is so rich and so accomplished," the field mouse told her.
"His house is much larger than mine. But he cannot bear the sun
or beautiful flowers, and speaks slightingly of them, as he has
never seen them."

Thumbelina had to sing to him. She sang "Lady-bird, lady-bird,
fly away home!" and other songs so prettily that the mole fell in love
with her; but he did not say anything, for he was very cautious.

There was a long underground tunnel he had dug from his house to his neighbor's and he invited the field mouse and Thumbelina to walk there with him. He held in his mouth a piece of phosphorescent wood which glowed like fire, and led them through the long dark passage. At one point, they came to a place where a dead swallow lay. The poor bird had evidently died of cold. Thumbelina was saddened by the sight, for she remembered the little birds that had sung so beautifully to her all summer.

But the mole kicked him with his bandy legs and said, "He can't sing now! It must be terrible to be a little bird! Birds *always* starve in winter."

"Yes, that is true," agreed the field mouse.

Thumbelina did not say anything; but when the other two had passed on
she bent down to the bird and kissed his closed eyes gently. "Perhaps it
was he that sang to me so prettily last summer," she thought. "How
much pleasure he gave me, dear little bird!"

Thumbelina could not sleep that night. She got out of bed and wove
a great big blanket of straw. This she carried off to spread over the dead
bird, and piled upon it thistledown as soft as cotton wool.

"Farewell, pretty bird!" she said. "Farewell, and thank you for your
beautiful songs in the summer." Then she lay her head on the bird's
chest. To her surprise the bird was not dead! He had been frozen, but
with the warmth Thumbelina had provided, he came to life again.

Thumbelina trembled with fright. The bird seemed very
large to her, as she was only an inch high.
But he was so ill...

The next night she crept out to see him again. He was alive but very weak. The swallow could only open his eyes for a moment and look at Thumbelina.

"Thank you," he said. "I feel so much better! Soon I shall be strong and will be able to fly again in the warm sunshine."

"But it is winter outside," she said. "Stay in your warm bed and I will take care of you!"

Thumbelina brought the swallow water in a flower, which he drank. He then told her how one of his wings had been torn on a bramble, so that he could not keep up with the other swallows as they flew away to warmer lands. At last he had dropped down exhausted—he could remember no more.

The whole winter Thumbelina nursed the swallow tenderly.

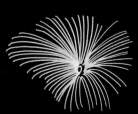

The spring came, the sun warmed the earth again and one day Thumbelina opened a hole in the roof of the tunnel. The swallow prepared to leave and offered the tiny girl a ride on his back if she wanted to go with him. But Thumbelina reluctantly declined, for she knew the field mouse would be sad if she left.

"Farewell then, dear little girl!" said the swallow, and flew off into the sunshine. Thumbelina gazed after him with tears in her eyes.

"Thumbelina!" cried the field mouse, soon after.
"Our neighbor has proposed to you! What a
piece of luck! Now you must start to make
your wedding dress! It must be special
if you are to become the wife of our
splendid friend the mole!"

Thumbelina had to spin all day
long, and the field mouse hired four
spiders who wove day and night.
Every evening the mole visited.

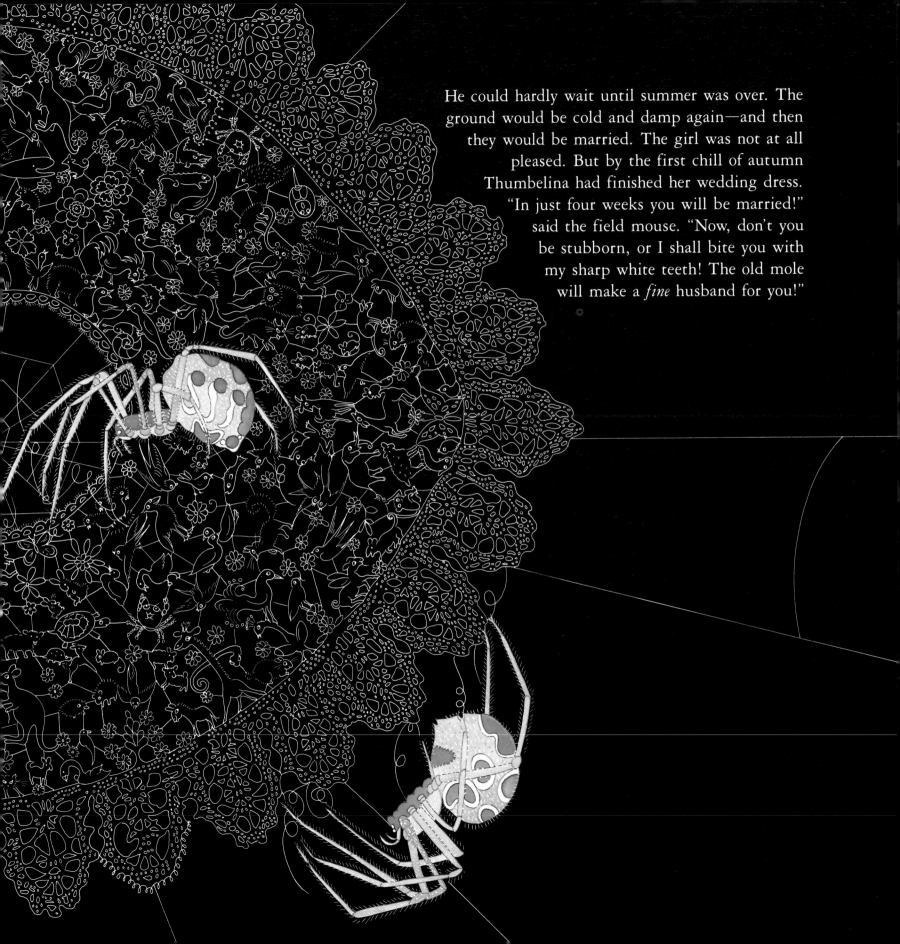

He could hardly wait until summer was over. The
ground would be cold and damp again—and then
they would be married. The girl was not at all
pleased. But by the first chill of autumn
Thumbelina had finished her wedding dress.
"In just four weeks you will be married!"
said the field mouse. "Now, don't you
be stubborn, or I shall bite you with
my sharp white teeth! The old mole
will make a *fine* husband for you!"

The wedding day arrived. The mole had come to fetch Thumbelina to live with him deep under the ground, never to come out again. The poor little girl ran outside to say goodbye to the beautiful sun.

"Farewell, farewell!" she said, and put her arms around a little red flower. "Give my love to the dear swallow when you see him!"

And then, "Tweet, tweet!" sounded in her ear. Thumbelina looked up to see the swallow swooping down to her. She told him how unhappy she was to have to marry the ugly old mole, and then she burst into tears.

"The cold winter is coming again," said the swallow. "I must fly to warmer lands. Will you come with me now? You can sit on my back, and we will fly far away from the ugly mole and his dark house—over the mountains, to countries where the sun shines more brightly than here —where it is always summer, and there are always beautiful flowers. Do come with me, dear little Thumbelina. You saved my life when I lay frozen in the dark tunnel!"

"Yes! Yes! I will," cried Thumbelina, and got up on the swallow's back, placing her feet on one of his outstretched wings.

Up into the air he flew, over woods and seas, and over great snowy mountains. She crept under his feathers to keep warm—her head out only enough to admire the beautiful things below.

At last they came to warm lands where the sun *was* brighter and the sky seemed twice as high. Green and purple grapes hung in the hedges. In the woods grew oranges and lemons, and the air was scented with myrtle and mint. Under the splendid green trees beside a blue lake stood a glittering white marble castle. There were many swallow's nests among the turrets, and in one of these lived the swallow who carried Thumbelina.

"Here is my house!" he said. "But it won't please you. I will set you down so you can find a home for yourself in one of those lovely flowers below."

"Splendid!" said she, clapping her little hands.

Thumbelina chose a perfect white lily. The swallow flew down and sat her upon one of its broad leaves. To her astonishment, a tiny little man was standing in the middle of the flower! He had a golden crown on his head, the most beautiful wings on his shoulders, and he himself was no bigger than Thumbelina. He was the King of All the Flowers.

"How handsome he is!" thought Thumbelina. And seeing Thumbelina, the young king was delighted, for she was the most beautiful girl he had ever seen. He took the golden crown from his head and put it on hers. He asked her name, and if she would be his wife— Queen of All the Flowers.

Now here was a different kind of husband than an ugly toad or a dreary mole. Thumbelina said, "Yes!"

Then the rest of the flowers popped open and fairies came out bearing gifts for Thumbelina. The *best* was
a pair of silvery wings, which was fastened to her back, so that now she *too* could fly from flower
to flower. Everyone wished them joy, and the swallow circled overhead, singing sweetly.
"Farewell, farewell!" he said, as he flew away—far, far away, back to Denmark.
There he shared a cozy little nest above a window with his wife,
who can tell fairy stories. "Tweet, tweet!" he sang to her.
And that is the way we learned the whole story.